Sweetcorn Suzie

Janice Wee

Published by Janice Wee, 2024.

This is a work of fiction. Similarities to real people, places, or events are entirely coincidental.

SWEETCORN SUZIE

First edition. February 20, 2024.

ISBN: 979-8224953530

Written by Janice Wee.

Also by Janice Wee

Emunah Chronicles
Disturbing Dreams
The Quest For Immortality
The Beast's Mark
The Quest For Immortality
The Characters & Events in The Quest for Immortality

Short Stories from Long Hill
Chico & Yvette
Escape To Long Hill

Tales From Singapore
Singapore's Runaway
Two Worlds, One Love & a Serial Killer
Naughty Little Nonya
Little Nonya's Escapades

Standalone

Escape

Sweetcorn Suzie

Watch for more at www.janicewee.com.

Table of Contents

Dedicated to all the women out there who blunder their way through life's challenges.

Fire Safety

"Girls!"

Melons bouncing, Miss Melody, our Home Economics teacher, raised her voice over the chaos.

"Don't ever do this."

Fire blazed, frightening us thirteen-year-old girls in our first cooking class. Cool as a cucumber, Miss Melody took the pan of burning oil from our classmate's trembling hand and set it in the middle the concrete kitchen floor.

"Remember girls," Miss Melody emphasised as she filled a bucket with water.

"Do not try this."

Our hearts pounding with morbid curiosity, we stood fixated. We couldn't tear our eyes off our teacher as she carried the pail full of water, striding towards the flaming oil.

"Stand back," she ordered - an unnecessary command. We weren't stupid. All of us had the sense to stay as far from the fire as we could.

Bracing herself, several feet away from the pan of flames, she flung the water at the burning oil, putting it out. It was a miracle the heated oil had not splashed on her, or any of us, for that matter. We were fortunate to escape unscathed.

"This is an example of what NOT to do when the oil catches fire," she concluded, stunning her impressionable audience.

SO, IF THIS IS WHAT we should not do, then what can we do if oil catches fire?

Since we were already on the subject of fire safety, she proceeded to lecture us about the hazard fire posed in the kitchen. She used the recent accidents from other less fortunate classes to illustrate the dangers of fire.

That was back when schools still used gas ovens. One girl poked her head too deep into the oven when she lit it, setting her own eyebrows aflame.

By the end of our class, every single girl had the importance of fire safety drilled deep into her psyche. In simple terms. We were traumatised for life.

Thanks to that fateful class, I've harboured a deep fear of gas-fuelled appliances, which annoyed my mother to no end.

What I hated was the fact that we used a gas-powered water heater for our showers. To switch it on, you light the gas with a ***pop*** so that dancing tongues of fire heat our bath water. Mom never understood why whenever I switched on the water heater, I'd scream and duck.

To make matters worse, we cooked on gas stoves. My only consolation was that we had those gas-lighting guns and didn't have to use matches.

I lit gas fires the same way many of my former classmates from that fateful home economics class would.

Turn on the gas.

Spark it ablaze with the gun.

Duck for cover when it "explodes".

It's one of my quirks my mom couldn't fathom with. All thanks to that memorable fire safety class my classmates and I endured at the tender age of thirteen.

The years flew by. I grew up, got married, and moved to my own home with my husband.

From day one, I was adamant against gas powered appliances. Everything had to run on electricity. At least that's what I wanted but not what public housing we lived in provided for.

We had a gas stove which I used for a season with much trepidation. Over the years, I switched to the electric oven, electric slow cooker, electric rice pot and electric kettle for all my cooking needs.

That's safe right?

Not when you're a complete klutz with two left hands and two left feet.

I was home alone, preparing dinner for my family.

All was going well, when absentminded me touched the unprotected heating element with my oven glove.

That angry red glow should have served as a warning, but that didn't register to this bumbling blur queen.

MY OVEN GLOVE CAUGHT fire. In one horrific moment,

flames shot up.

I thought I was a goner.

Suddenly, the jagged edge of the flames flattened. It looked like an enormous invisible hand slammed down the fire, putting it out.

The flames charred the top of my oven glove but the inside which protected my hand stayed intact. I was unscathed. I didn't even feel the heat of the fire, thanks to that miraculous rescue.

I kept the charred oven glove for years and continued using it as a reminder of what happened. Numerous washes have removed the blackened portion, but it served as proof to me what I saw was not a product of my imagination.

My God, who at times is my only friend, stepped in to protect me.

Or maybe He assigned a guardian angel to protect me.

I can only imagine the details because while you may observe the wind's effects, you can't see the wind itself. Likewise, I'm unable to catch even a glimpse of my protector. I can only witness the results of that protection.

Double Agent

"The walls have ears," Joe whispered as he brushed past me. He stared straight ahead, deliberately ignoring my presence, though he directed his words at me.

He spoke no more of this. As a matter of fact, I ceased to exist to him.

Sally too.

Once a friend, or so I thought, now she ignored me completely. Only once, when the office was half-empty, she responded. Terror mingled with worry danced in her eyes.

"We aren't in the same team anymore, so this will be our final conversation."

Huh?

Yeah, like that made a lot of sense.

But you know what was the weirdest?

Mary.

A strong and caring woman whom I had regarded as my mentor, treated me like her worst enemy.

That stung.

What did I do?

What happened?

"You dare show your face, after the nasty emails you sent to the boss about Mary?" Corba growled. He hated me and made no secret about it.

In a sick way, he wanted me to lord over me.

Mary intervened, stopping his harassment for a season.

For that brief period, I was happy – Tucked under her wing in the only sane place in that crazy organization.

Then came the altercation.

Next thing I knew, I was transferred out of Mary's team and forced to report to Corba.

It wasn't pleasant, to say the least. He hated my guts but wanted something from me.

What did he want?

Don't ask me.

I had absolutely no idea.

Half the time, I felt I was in some spy movie where everyone had some sort of hidden agenda.

Totally clueless, I'd stumbled through each workday, wondering if something was going on. Yet I had no idea what.

From then on, whenever I tried to speak with Mary, she'd turn her nose up with a "hmmph." She showed utter disdain towards me.

What happened?

She was the friend I respected most in the entire organization.

Yet she treated me like a foe. It broke my heart.

Over time, I came to realize that underneath all that hostility, it was but an act.

There was some conference which involved everyone but the two of us. I took that opportunity to approach her. The old

Mary, my big sister and mentor was back. She gave me pertinent advice in hushed tones, her eyes darted towards the door of that meeting room.

"Meeting's ended. They're coming out now," she stated. "Better go back."

She reverted to her ice-queen persona when we next met, but I took her advice to heart, watching my every step. Life went on. I tried to do all my tasks to the best of my ability, without her guidance. I missed her wisdom. Her friendship.

Days turned to weeks. Weeks became months.

Then one day, while I was in the lift, the door opened. She walked in. As usual, her eyes brimmed with hatred, her demeanor could give a girl a major frost bite.

The door closed.

It was just the two of us.

My mentor returned.

I faced numerous obstacles which I had no idea how to resolve. As we travelled down in the lift, she answered my burning questions, teaching me as much as she could in the short duration of that ride.

Ping!

The bell went off. She gestured at the door. Following her lead, I too put on my mask as we walked out the door, heading in opposite directions, posing as sworn enemies.

What was that about?

At that time, though I played along, I had no idea. One thing's certain. I was thoroughly sick and tired of the cloak and dagger work environment that belonged in an asylum and not a financial institution.

Much as I dreaded the toxic work environment each day, I couldn't quit.

I needed the job for the pittance of a salary I received. It wasn't enough to pay the bills but it was still better than nothing.

You see, my hubby had lost his job and I had to somehow support our family with our two growing boys, the helper who was still under contract, pay for the club and the car loan installments. As I walked home one day in misery, I cried to God, confiding in him all my problems. "God. How?"

God's answer came in an unexpected way. You see, I had started a website as a hobby. I needed pictures for it.

It was then that I discovered I could use professionally taken photographs from affiliate marketing networks[1]. When the content on my website called for pictures of women, for example, I'd display product images from clothing stores. That worked.

As a bonus, I could earn affiliate commissions such as from the clothing stores.

I got my first cheque.

A whopping 40 USD. After 15 USD or more bank charges, I had earned enough from months of hard work to buy a meal.

Whoopie!

Then something happened. For an unknown reason, my website took off. People were visiting my website, clicking on the affiliate links and buying the products. 40 USD became 400 USD.

The following month, I got 4000 USD for one month's work on the website.

That's far more than one month's salary from my full-time job!

Opportunity knocked.

I answered by quitting my toxic job.

The boss urged me to take back my resignation.

It was only then that the powers that be disclosed the truth.

I was but a pawn in a much larger scheme.

Someone had set up a trap for the boss, who headed the division, and who reported to the Chief Executive Officer. The boss knew about it and was using me to lure the culprit into complacency, so that he might get careless and would be easier to entrap.

It all began when someone spoofed my email address and sent nasty things about Mary to the boss. At first, the boss believed these emails came from me and trusted the information they conveyed. These emails got Mary into trouble. She, and everyone else, believed I had backstabbed her, which was why I was snubbed at work.

It appeared that it was but a test. The culprit had bigger fish to fry. His ultimate target was the boss.

The villain spoofed email addresses of top management. Unlike this blur queen, the senior management was shrewd. The boss knew his email had been spoofed and set a trap for the culprit, with me as the bait.

They wanted me to stay on to see this through. The only reward being that I'd finally know who had targeted me and I would be privy to the entire clandestine affair.

Mary, too, spoke to me, leveraging our friendship to get me to stay on. But by then, I really had enough. I couldn't take any more of that insanity, so I went through with my resignation.

I never found out what had happened. Who the culprit was. What his or her goal was but I have some idea.

Mary had a target on her back because of her position and standing in the company. She had a rival who wanted her out of the picture. It could have been that rival. Or it could have been someone else.

It was a highly political company with intrigue and rivalry everywhere. Palace politics reigned. The ambitious clawed their way up, stomping down whoever got in their way.

After that experience, I stayed away from corporate life for the next decade.

With the car, club, household bills, helper and two growing boys, and with my husband still jobless, how could we cope with both of us now unemployed?

For starters, I maintained my website and created new ones. Oh, I also prayed and pleaded with God to provide for us.

From nothing, our traffic ballooned with our web pages coming up tops in Google, Yahoo and MSN searches for the products we promoted. Our affiliate commissions went through the roof.

When the Israelites were in the desert those forty years, God rained Manna from heaven to feed them.

When both my husband and I were jobless with no way out, God rained money through our websites, giving us far more than we needed. We had plenty to feed and clothe our entire family, pay all our bills and splurge on luxuries. We spent the next few years as stay home dad and mom who were there for our kids during their critical childhood years.

Each month, the cheques came in. Their amounts were consistent. The total being far more than anything we could ever hope to get from salaried work. (Neither of us could command much in terms of salaries anyway). Month in, month out, my husband would look at the cheques and scratch his head. "Not possible."

I agreed. But we'd bank in the cheques anyway. God provided for us bountifully through those precious years.

Of Knives and Boys

We hang out with our family friends at holiday chalets pretty often. The grown-ups would have their own activities, leaving us kids to our own devices in one of these chalets. I was one of a few girls amongst the kids; in fact, most of the time, I was the only girl hanging out with the boys. I kept my hair short, dressed and acted like a boy to blend in. The boys in turn treated me like one of them.

In front of our parents, we'd don our halos and angelic expressions.

Wearing the most innocent smiles we could muster, we'd wave our parents goodbye as they deposited us in the "kid's chalet". Dylan and I were the oldest of the cohort. Angus was next in seniority.

The door closed.

Angus ran to the door and secured the lock. Turning to us with a devilish grin, he'd announce, "Pillow fight!"

We'd each grab a pillow and attack the nearest sucker.

Knowing we'd have to face our parents at the end of the night, we had one unbreakable rule – No visible injuries.

That led to the other rule in the game. No direct contact. All blows must be through a pillow or some form of bedding.

Angus would grab Wyatt and wrap the pillow around his head, boxing his ears through them. Like everyone else, I'd grab a pillow and plunge into a gratifying fight.

"Wait a minute," Chito, the newcomer exclaimed. "That's a girl!" He pointed at me.

I found my victim. I mean, opponent.

Thwack!

Pillow in hand I'd whack his head. Hard.

"Hey!"

Thwack!

Thwack!

Thwack!

"That's no girl," Chito sputtered.

"Told you," Dylan laughed while bashing Julius through the pillow, as per game rules.

Red-faced, pillow swung, my target's forgotten all decorum as he fought to avenge his pride.

Laughing, I'd block his blows with an arm, whacking his head with other, through a pillow of course, to disorientate him, so I could get more blows in.

Crash!

Everyone froze.

Dread suffocated us when what happened sunk in.

The chalet's desktop lamp laid on the ground.

Shattered.

Uh oh.

We were all in big trouble.

Some quick-thinking boy swept away the evidence while the rest of us huddled to figure out what to do next.

There was only one way out.

Halos on our heads, angelic expressions on our faces, we streamed out of the chalet, smiling, sweet as sugar, towards our parents.

So, there we were. Figuring out how to keep from dying of boredom, without destroying public property. Pillow fights were too risky. But arm wrestling?

Before you know it, we were arm wrestling one another. Losers drop out. Winners battle on.

Dylan, who was the same age as me, was an easy opponent to beat. He hadn't much in terms of arm strength. No one goes easy on me just because I'm a girl. In fact, no one regards me as a girl anyway. Not after I beat the sense out of anyone who doubted.

High from my victory, I took my place opposite Angus, a school swimmer, the strongest of the boys. He's very strong. But so was I.

Back in those days, I did push ups every day. The usual pushes with both hands, then one arm push ups on my side to train my triceps.

The match began. His brothers and cousins cheered me on.

Elbows supported on the table, with all my strength I pushed. He wouldn't go down. He might give an inch, then take it back as we both strained for what felt like hours.

Their cheers grew louder as the boys wanted to witness Angus beaten by a bona fide girl.

Bolstered by their support, in a moment of his weakness, in my final burst of strength, I pushed his arm all the way down.

I beat him!

I beat Angus!

I couldn't believe it but I did it.

That horrified look, the utter shock on his face, cemented my victory.

The room burst into cheers. It felt like Anfield when Liverpool wins a match.

I never agreed to a rematch. Ever.

It was by fluke I'd won. I also had the unfair advantage of age way back when we were still in our early teens.

Since then, I have married a swimmer who has rarely (or maybe never) been beaten in arm wrestling, so if Angus ever asks for a rematch, I know I can count on my hubby to represent me. Then again, I wouldn't want to introduce my guy to my gang. He's under the impression I'm sweet and feminine and I'd like to keep that illusion intact.

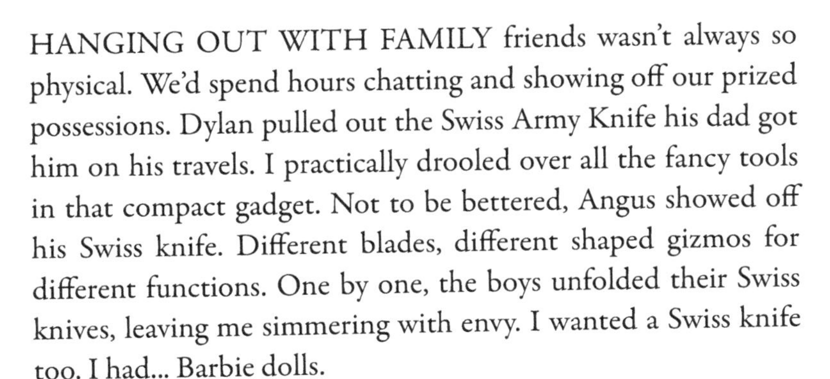

HANGING OUT WITH FAMILY friends wasn't always so physical. We'd spend hours chatting and showing off our prized possessions. Dylan pulled out the Swiss Army Knife his dad got him on his travels. I practically drooled over all the fancy tools in that compact gadget. Not to be bettered, Angus showed off his Swiss knife. Different blades, different shaped gizmos for different functions. One by one, the boys unfolded their Swiss knives, leaving me simmering with envy. I wanted a Swiss knife too. I had... Barbie dolls.

On a trip with my family to Europe, I finally had my chance. With my allowance, I bought a Swiss Army Knife that I could afford. Needless to say, it became my most prized possession. I had no idea how to use it, but I carried it with me everywhere I went, with pride.

Walking through customs at the airport with my treasure in my waist pouch, the alarms went off. The security officer asked me to step aside. There, I surrendered my waist pouch and a lady officer patted me down. Turned out that my Swiss knife was the culprit. Lesson learnt. Keep Swiss knives in the checked baggage.

One reason I have never used my Swiss Army Knife was that I'm a clumsy coward.

Besides tripping on my own two feet, knives and tools tend to slip when I use them.

I dare not even clean a blender knowing the chances I end up with bloodied hands are in the ninety-percentile.

I used to cook Nonya food. Each dish required ten to twenty shallots either pounded or ground to a smooth pulp. Mom bought me a blender set. She said the modern Nonya doesn't use the mortar and pestle anymore. Everyone dumps the peeled shallots and other ingredients into the blender. Turn it on. A minute later, it's ready for frying.

"Thanks Mom," I'd reply politely. Then the blender and its mini companion got chucked into the cupboard, untouched for the next three decades. One fine day, the blender committed suicide. When I opened the cupboard door, it fell from its perch and shattered upon impact.

Rest in peace, old friend.

I swept up its remains and dumped it down the rubbish chute. ☹

Although it had never ever been used, it had been my constant companion in the kitchen throughout the decades. Albeit a silent one!

When one cooks, it's impossible to escape the use of kitchen knives. I chopped fruits and vegetables with much trepidation.

I was home alone, preparing dinner for my family.

My mind strayed while I chopped the vegetables.

That's when my right hand misjudged and sent the blade down, towards the fingers of my left.

Before the metal could touch my hand, I felt an invisible person flick the chopper out of my grip. The knife landed neatly in the kitchen sink. I was completely unharmed.

I know it was my God.

Did He protect me Himself?

Did he send a guardian angel?

I had no idea. All I could do was thanked my hidden protector, composed myself, then continued preparing dinner.

Chopping vegetables

Knife slips

An invisible hand flicks it away

Knife lands
safely in
sink

Of Bees and Poop

F*lush!*

Relief.

Like Daddy always said. A good poop is one of the sweetest joys in life. It's something you'd never appreciate unless you've had serious constipation. Hence the constant supply of sweet ripe bananas in my parents' home.

I was engrossed in my work when my colleague, one of the Boss's pets stormed up to me.

Livid.

Pointing at me, she hurled her accusations with Boss backing her every word – the biased judge and jury.

"She shitted all over the floor," the sycophant fumed. "I had to clean up her poop!"

I did what?

I was pretty sure I laid my eggs in the toilet bowl. You can't miss if you're sitting on the nest.

All my life, once I'd outgrown diapers, I've never pooped out of the bowl or hole or whatever. My Mom would certainly let me know if I ever absentmindedly dropped an egg out of place.

"Then she stepped on it and I had to clean up all the footsteps of shit!" Miss Sycophant ranted on.

Boss looked utterly disgusted at me. Sycophant was so convincing, she had me doubt my sanity. A sound reprimand and shaming later, I was back at my desk, continuing my work, though utterly miserable. High and mighty Sycophant mocked me with her smug triumphant smile.

Being underpaid was one thing. Being at the bottom of the ladder without any friends was still tolerable. But being picked on, targeted by Boss's pets?

To say I was upset would have been an understatement. I could only swallow my anger and quietly continue working at the computer.

In my heart, I cried to God, the only one who'd listen. Who'd understand.

What's wrong with me.

How is it possible I could poop on the floor and not realise it. How could I not realise I stepped on poop and smeared it everywhere?

Wait a minute. My shoes were clean. But no one would believe me. No one would dare speak against Boss's pets.

Then again, was I so mindless I did all that and not realise it?

Was I losing my mind?

With tears in my eyes, I continued my daily tasks, complaining to God. Asking him whether there's something wrong with me.

Then I heard a scream followed by a commotion in the office.

It was Miss Sycophant.

There was a large insect buzzing around her. Sycophant kept screaming while boss fussed over her precious pet.

Turned out the bee had stung Miss Sycophant's mouth.

I guess that's God's way of showing me He's vindicated me. Only God knows Miss Sycophant had been lying all along. And that is enough for me.

Vision of Heaven

With a heavy heart, I trudged towards my in-law's I called my weekday home.

Desperate for a job, I took a hefty pay cut. Fruit was a luxury I could not afford for myself. Everything I earned had to go to support our young family. To pay our bills. No luxuries for me. That didn't stop me from window shopping for bargains. That's how I struck gold.

I found a bag of bruised fruit at the supermarket. They were overripe and bruised but still good. Overjoyed, I bought the fruit and hid my loot in my bag, terrified I'd be discovered. I didn't want to surrender my precious fruit to the matriarch so that she could turn it into fruit juice for herself and her hubby.

Scattered streetlamps lit the path as I plodded through the darkness.

Mesmerized, I watched an aperture with glowing edges appear in front of me, like a porthole peeking into another world. That window grew larger and larger until it occupied most of my vision. I saw my mansion in heaven!

That was my house!

Okay, house sounds wrong. Palace would be more appropriate.

It had white walls and a roof made of clear, flawless rose quartz. I found myself floating towards it. Within its doors was a massive hall.

There were no individual bricks or separate tiles.

Each wall was made from a single white precious stone I couldn't identify. The flooring was definitely rose quartz - the gemstone I adore.

The precious stones my future home's made of are flawless. Perfect.

I could sense my Lord Jesus beside me although I did not see him. He revealed the mansion which he prepared for me.

Then it dawned on me that this beautiful home was empty. No furniture, no furnishings. It reminded me of a newly built home that's not ready for occupants just yet.

This world is not my home. I'm only passing through. That mansion is the eternal home Jesus prepared for me in Heaven, but it's not ready for me to move into. In other words, it's not yet my time.

It made the most impressive houses I've ever seen look pathetic in comparison. That's where you'll find me one day, when my time here on earth is over.

In this world where we live, my bathroom is my haven. I love to de-stress in a long shower. A bathtub is a luxury I could not afford.

I know of a beautiful sunken jacuzzi that functioned as the bathtub in a rich man's house. The matriarch would luxuriate in it.

Guess what?

I visited the bathroom in my heavenly mansion. It was made entirely of that same white gemstone, from a single unbroken piece. The stone is more precious than marble, translucent and flawless. In the center of it was a sunken bathtub, like a spacious private jacuzzi without the bubbles. The still water looked so inviting yet I sensed I was only allowed to look but not touch. How I longed to soak in it.

Another weird thing?

There was no toilet bowl.

Does that mean no one has to pee or poop in heaven?

Do we eat?

If we eat, what happens to the food when we're done?

The next thing I knew, I was back on that dark lonely path to my temporal home.

I couldn't get my mind off the mansion I had seen in my vision. What was that gorgeous white gemstone the walls were made of? It's not marble. It's pure white, translucent and glowed with innate beauty.

Going through a lifestyle magazine, my eyes fell on the gemstone set in a necklace an article showcased. That was moonstone. It wasn't even as beautiful or flawless as the flooring of my future home but I'm pretty sure that's what the floor of my mansion would be made of.

It's kind of ironical. I used to love gemstones.

After that vision, whenever I looked at displays of expensive gemstone jewelry, the unbidden thought pops up, declaring that these precious stones aren't even good enough for the flooring of our promised mansions.

Those jewels worn to flaunt earthly wealth are third grade - no better than discarded chips of flooring or building materials used for our homes in heaven.

Topsy Turvy Techie

"The numbers still don't tally," Mandy, my team leader pointed out. A warm-hearted woman with a brilliant mind, Mandy was the glue that held the team together.

I'd worked on the computer program for months. The logic was correct. The result ASS[2] yielded was consistently incorrect. I was at my wits' end.

Each of us had our own area of responsibilities based on our technical expertise so I couldn't expect her to figure out what's wrong with my codes.

Hubert, the smartest guy in our team suggested I discard my work and start again from scratch utilizing a different approach altogether. As stubborn as a mule, unable to resist an intriguing puzzle, I chose to ignore his advice and continue puzzling over the program I had written.

"There was a software upgrade. Maybe the new version is buggy?" I pointed out, to my own detriment.

The ASS consultant defended his software with great vehemence. He insisted it was perfect. ASS tested the modifications thoroughly so that any bugs in the rolled-out version would be impossible.

On hindsight, I should have followed Hubert's advice.

I was eventually transferred to another team with a supervisor who lacked any form of human compassion, Prudence Selfsworth, who in turn reported to Felicity Cowardine.

In that new team, one thing led to another, and I was fired.

"Please. I've got a family to feed." My eyes misted up with tears, I begged Prudence and her weasel of a boss, Felicity, to give me a chance to let me hold on to my job. I had told them that my husband was unemployed and still unable to find a job. We had two small children to provide for.

It broke me. I didn't know what I could possibly do without my job. Once upon a time, we had our own internet business. But I burnt out. It crashed. I couldn't resuscitate it no matter how hard I tried. I had no other option but to cling on to this job.

But those cold-hearted snakes couldn't care less. There was not an ounce of compassion in their eyes. It could have been my imagination but did I see a sadistic gleam in Prudence Selfsworth's eyes? I knew she didn't like me. It was obvious that me getting fired delighted her.

God is good. All the time.

To my surprise, not only did I find a new job rather quickly, but that position was also a big promotion on all fronts. I oversaw a massive project with a budget that would made my ex-company drool.

In my new role, my schedule was almost always more than double-booked, so a typical day at work would mean rushing from one meeting to another, declining most of the invites to meetings and cherry picking the ones to attend.

The vendor presentations for my project were crucial meetings I could not miss. I had to pick the best with all the information presented to me and knowledge I had gathered outside of these meetings.

Panting for breath, I barged into the meeting with as much dignity as I could muster – which was closed to zero. At least I didn't trip over my own two feet and fall flat on my face when I entered the room, so that's considered a win.

The chairperson insisted that the presenters wait for me as that project was my baby, so to speak. I was to make the final decision on which of the shortlisted vendors would be awarded the job.

There was a hushed silence as I entered the room. I looked at the panel of presenters, as I muttered an apology for being late. My heart skipped a beat as my eyes fell on their shocked expressions.

Seated and waiting to pitch for the project were the bosses who fired me – Prudence, my previous, heartless supervisor. Felicity, the weasel who shamelessly fired me and their clueless boss. Talk about coming around a full circle.

I made my decision. Their competition had the better solution. ☺

I had kept in touch with some ex-colleagues from Mandy's team and eventually learnt the full story.

As you know, I lost my job because I couldn't fix the computer program that was written in ASS.

I COULDN'T GET MY PROGRAM to work because ASS itself was buggy. They rolled out a software update which affected my program, making it produce the wrong results.

Apparently, I wasn't the only programmer affected. Many others were fired for the bugs in their programs before ASS finally admitted their mistake. In a sense, that gave me the final closure for that chapter of my life.

Woman's Problem

The bosses sat around the table. I had to be there to represent my team but the pain in my abdomen was hard to ignore.

"You look pale," Yvette, a compassionate lady boss turned to me, drawing unwanted attention my way.

Bracing myself, I mumbled. "I'm okay."

"If you aren't feeling well, go see a doctor. You can get someone from your team to represent your interests," she wasn't buying my act.

My stomach spasmed. I doubled over.

"Go to A&E now," my boss insisted. "We'll get someone to cover you." He refused to take no for an answer.

Steeling myself, I forced on a smile, excused myself and walked to the Accident & Emergency Department across the road.

Though my pain tolerance is very high, it wasn't easy ignoring the pain as I made my way to the counter. Immediately, they put me in a wheelchair and sent me to the Critical Care Unit. I texted family and friends, asking them to intercede for me in prayer. I still texted my own team and colleagues in other departments, coordinating. Telling them what had to be done, working even from the bed even as I wrestled with the pain until dear Mindy, a friend of mine who headed another department, scolded me. She told me to stop. She'd cover for me.

By then, pain came not in waves but at an agonizing fever pitch. Relentless. I had given birth to two babies naturally, without painkillers. While the pain from childbirth is reputed to be the worst, the torment I experienced by the time they wheeled me in a bed, exceeded the climax of labour pains.

I lost all sense of time, curled into a ball, trying to find relief from the never-ending agony. The nurses inserted tubes into my hand. I found out later that they had to drip two different types of antibiotics into my bloodstream. The infection had gone so far, it's a hit or miss thing. If that combination of antibiotics work, I'll live. If not, then I'll meet my Maker.

I'm not sure how, but I finally fell asleep. Maybe they sedated me? I can't imagine how I could have slept through those cramping spasms.

Morning broke.

I awoke.

The pain was gone.

The antibiotics worked.

I survived.

For an entire week, they took blood from me every single day. Sometimes as many as thrice a day if whoever drew blood had not taken enough for the necessary tests. I have a phobia of needles. When I was in labour, I refused the epidural, kicking away anyone who approached me with the sinister syringe. The nurses thought I was extremely brave until they drew blood from me. I almost fainted.

Anyway, there's no escaping needles this time. There was one perpetually stuck into the vein at the back of my hand so they could administer a drip on short notice. What I dreaded even more was the daily blood test.

Needles aside, the rest of my hospital stay felt like a staycation. With the pain gone, I could receive visitors. Read. Sleep.

Sneak out of my bed when the nurses weren't looking to go shopping.

I wasn't as bad as you might think. I'd leave a note on my pillow promising to be back soon.

The week breezed by. I had the bed rest I so desperately needed. The doctors told me what happened. I had an infection near my uterus. My ovaries were scarred but that's normal with stress. After the long explanation about infection in that woman's area, and the fear of getting my Intrauterine Device infected, I opted to have my birth control removed. Which meant, no more protection.

My hospitalization leave was split into two phases. For the first week, I stayed in the hospital for monitoring. The second week was home rest where they trusted I'd be in good hands and get the rest I needed for full recovery.

"Honey, I'm home," I walked through the door into the waiting arms of my hubby. He gave me a memorable welcome - he impregnated me the first day of my home stay.

How did I know?

A missed period and a positive test from the home kit confirmed my suspicion. Our third baby's on the way!

The ultrasound scan showed a cluster of cells. Since we haven't figured a name yet for the child, we stuck to that moniker.

When they scanned my ovaries, out of curiosity, I asked the sonographer the state of my ovaries.

"They're fine," she replied as she continued scanning.

"I was told there's a scar," I was puzzled.

"There's no scar. They are perfect. As new as a baby's ovaries," she retorted.

Now that was weird. How did my scarred ovaries suddenly become as good as new? Then again, my immediate pregnancy had to be testament that my ovaries were in great shape, I reasoned.

I had just recovered from a life-threatening infection and was on powerful antibiotics when I conceived. I was already in my forties, so to be honest, Cluster of Cells never stood a chance.

Initially, I was hopeful. Baby grew as expected with each medical appointment. Then on the tenth week, the doctor broke the news. By now, the heart should be beating but there's no heartbeat.

On top of that, the baby hadn't grown since the eighth week checkup. In other words, Cluster of Cells died at eight weeks in my womb.

I grieved. Couldn't believe it.

The doctor advised me to wash out my womb. If not, I'd be carrying the dead fetus in until my body expels it on its own, piece by piece which can be horrific.

I asked for time, but it all happened exactly as my doctor had said.

I bled. My body was expelling the dead unborn child. I went to the hospital and let them clean out my womb, knowing in my heart, my baby had gone home to be with the Lord. I committed my unborn child to God's hands, letting go. If God chose to take

CoC home, it would have been for the little one's best interests. I had no support for this baby. No one wanted this risky child.

Considering the circumstances of the conception, the chances Cluster of Cells would be born deformed, were very high. My dad promised to take care of the baby, but other than having Daddy's support, I'd be fighting for my baby alone and already, I was struggling. I fell into depression and sought treatment.

A year later, when my contract ended, my boss decided to let me go. It was a huge blow. When I was hired, the Human Resources lady told me that I had to close every trace of my online business within six months, but after the contract ends, I'd be converted to a permanent staff. Believing her, I closed my business. I had nothing left to fall back on if my employer were to renegade on that verbal promise.

So, there I was. I lost my baby. After giving up my business, I lost my job. So, what now?

I couldn't afford treatment for depression, so I stopped treatment, stopping the meds when I ran out. But strangely, my depression lifted.

What next?

My father passed away in the next year. He fought the good fight and had gone home to be with the Lord. My children were devastated. Kindly Grandpa was everyone's favorite grandparent.

In a strange way, I found comfort. Cluster of Cells wasn't up there alone. The best grandparent ever, my Daddy, had gone to be with the Lord where CoC was already waiting. When I was down, I'd imagine Daddy cradling CoC.

I really hope Daddy gave my baby a proper name – something better than Cluster of Cells.

I take comfort in the fact that one day, when my time is up, we'll be reunited in paradise.

What can I do? There's no way out.
Maybe you could
So how did it go?
Okay I guess. She forgot all about it.
I'm so dead! What do I do now?
I'm sure there's a way
Why are you worried? Everytime you hit insurmountable problems, they disappear suddenly. Your God always bails you out.

Psalms 23

(A Psalm of David.)

The LORD is my shepherd; I shall not want.

He maketh me to lie down in green pastures: he leadeth me beside the still waters.

He restoreth my soul: he leadeth me in the paths of righteousness for his name's sake.

Yea, though I walk through the valley of the shadow of death, I will fear no evil: for thou art with me; thy rod and thy staff they comfort me.

Thou preparest a table before me in the presence of mine enemies: thou anointest my head with oil; my cup runneth over.

Surely goodness and mercy shall follow me all the days of my life: and I will dwell in the house of the LORD for ever.

---

[1] Affiliate marketing is an arrangement where an online retailer pays commission for traffic or sales generated from referrals by the external websites who partner with it.

[2] ASS stands for Analytical Statistics System, a software suite by a fictitious company. (I'm not using real names here or any further identifying details.)

Don't miss out!

Visit the website below and you can sign up to receive emails whenever Janice Wee publishes a new book. There's no charge and no obligation.

https://books2read.com/r/B-A-BTWW-FDYTC

BOOKS 2 READ

Connecting independent readers to independent writers.

Did you love *Sweetcorn Suzie*? Then you should read *Little Nonya's Escapades*[1] by Janice Wee!

[2]

Tammy's a teacher's kid. Everyone had high expectations of her in the exam-obsessed country where she lived. But Tammy had a secret. Her mind played tricks on her when she read. To make matters worse, she's a Peranakan who had to take Chinese exams. Mandarin, a foreign language to her was the native tongue of her rivals in class.On top of that, Tammy seemed to have a large part of her brain missing - the part that's supposed to hold common sense.Join ditzy, klutzy Tammy as she navigates through School's challenges, rabid younger kids and wayward shuttlecocks as she

1. https://books2read.com/u/3LjoN1

2. https://books2read.com/u/3LjoN1

and her cousins drive the adults up the wall.This book is a must read for parents with young school-going kids, more than for the kids themselves.It also contains the study strategies of a hopeless ditz of a kid who topped her class in exams.

Read more at www.janicewee.com.

Also by Janice Wee

Emunah Chronicles
Disturbing Dreams
The Quest For Immortality
The Beast's Mark
The Quest For Immortality
The Characters & Events in The Quest for Immortality

Short Stories from Long Hill
Chico & Yvette
Escape To Long Hill

Tales From Singapore
Singapore's Runaway
Two Worlds, One Love & a Serial Killer
Naughty Little Nonya
Little Nonya's Escapades

Standalone

Escape

Sweetcorn Suzie

Watch for more at www.janicewee.com.

About the Author

Janice Wee is Straits Born Chinese from Singapore.

She is a sixth generation Singaporean, the daughter of two English teachers and who spent her childhood in libraries.

Learn more about the worlds and characters in her stories in her website janicewee.com

Read more at www.janicewee.com.